TISSUE, PLEASE!

by
Lisa Kopelke

SIMON & SCHUSTER BOOKS FOR YOUNG READERS
NEW YORK LONDON TORONTO SYDNEY

SIMON & SCHUSTER BOOKS FOR YOUNG READERS
An imprint of Simon & Schuster Children's Publishing Division
1230 Avenue of the Americas, New York, New York 10020
SIMON & SCHUSTER BOOKS FOR YOUNG READERS is a trademark of Simon & Schuster, Inc.
Book design by Greg Stadnyk
The text for this book is set in Green and Neo Neo.
The illustrations for this book are rendered in acrylic.
Manufactured in China
2 4 6 8 10 9 7 5 3 1
Library of Congress Cataloging-in-Publication Data
Kopelke, Lisa.
Tissue, please! / by Lisa Kopelke.—1st ed.
p. cm.
Summary: At school, dance rehearsal, and home Frog and his friends sniff when their
noses run, until Frog's parents show him how much better it is to use a tissue.
ISBN 0-689-86248-2
[1. Frogs—Fiction. 2. Behavior—Fiction. 3. Etiquette—Fiction.] I. Title.
PZ7.K83614 Ti 2004
[E]—dc22   2003012235

To Claire

Thanks for your inspiration!

Miss Jordan's ballet class, the students and staff at TBS, and Jamie Dick and the kids of Desert Spring Arts.

Frog and his friends did *everything* together.

At recess they played hopscotch
and jumped rope together.

In class they sat at the same table and studied together. And when they had runny noses, they sniffled and snuffled together.

"**Snerrrfle!**" they announced as they wiped their noses on their arms.
"**Ahem!**" Mr. Sage replied.

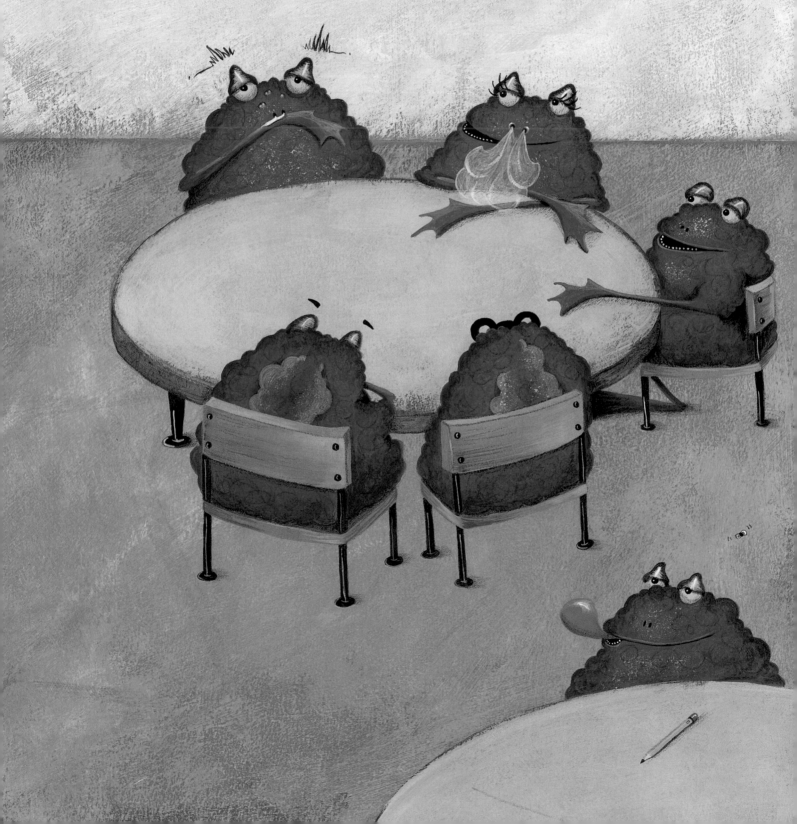

After school Frog and his friends rode
their bikes to dance class together.
They were practicing for their recital.

Frog loved his ballet class.

Lately he had a hard time concentrating. He still had a runny nose, which made it difficult to dance.

"Schnorrrkle!" Frog rang out.

When his friends heard him, they remembered their noses were runny too. Soon the whole class was one huge chorus of sniffles and snuffles as they wiped their noses on their arms.

Miss Tutu was so disgusted, all she could say was "Yuck!"

At home Frog was enjoying his dinner: potato-bug soup with fish crackers. He was in the middle of a big slurp when he realized he needed to sniffle.

"Snerrrf—" Frog started.

"That's not polite at the dinner table," interrupted his father.

Frog's mother leaped out of the room and came back with a box of tissues.

"Please, use this instead,"
she suggested.

Frog blew his nose into the tissue and was amazed
at how well it worked. His nose felt great!

"And here is an extra to keep in your pocket,"

added his father,

"just in case."

It was the day of the big dance recital. Frog and his friends jumped across the stage into place.

The crowd "Ooooohed" as the curtain rose.

In the middle of his grand plié Frog's nose began to run again. So he sniffled. It didn't work.

Frog was getting ready for a gigantic snuffle, when he noticed his teacher watching him offstage.

Frog suddenly remembered . . . a tissue!

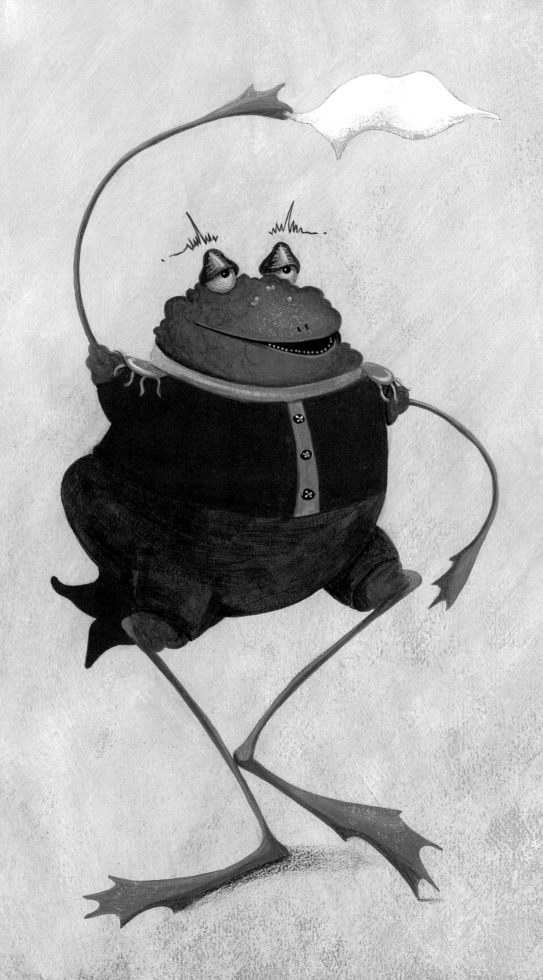

Frog quickly hopped over and took
a tissue out of the box on the
piano and hopped back into place.
He blew his nose and finished his
plié in one grand move, waving
the tissue high above his head.

Frog's friends were inspired.

They each pirouetted across the stage,
grabbing a tissue mid-twirl.

"Mmmmmmmpfff,"
they blew in a loud symphony.

Then one by one they waved their tissues over their heads, danced over, and flung them into the trash.

Miss Tutu was so proud, all she could say was
"Bravo!"

The audience was impressed.
"Encore!" they yelled.

And from that day on the *Dance of the Tissue-Box Fairies* was the big finale of every dance recital.